Jack, Skinny Bones, and the Golden Pancakes

by
M.C. Helldorfer

illustrated by
Elise Primavera

VIKING

ow this happened in dry country, down where the river is nothing but a stream of dust blowing through Hell's Canyon and the town of Prickly Pear. On the edge of Prickly Pear lived an orphan boy named Jack. When Jack was just a babe, he was left in the desert with nothing but a diaper and two cactus needles to hold it on.

Skinny Bones found him.

The old yellow dog had run away from Granny Trick. He was belly-crawling through the desert and thirsty enough to drink up a river and two ponds, but nothing, *nothing* would make him go back to the old lady. Then he heard little Jack cry. He saw big balls of dust rolling down Jack's baby cheeks. Skinny Bones turned around and carried the boy home.

PRICKLY Pear THAT-A-WAY

If you call Granny's place a home—I don't, for she was a sneaky old woman and hot-tempered as a pepper. Granny made her money selling snakeskin belts. She sold them cheap. But no sooner was your money in her pocket than that pretty thing'd get to untying itself and slithering down your leg. Your pants got to going after that.

And it was no good stirring up a fuss about it. Granny would always fuss more, then make it up nice, selling you some fine lizard-skin shoes. Of course, they'd walk away without you.

Oh, the old lady was full of tricks. About the only thing she didn't figure on was little Jack watching and learning her every one. Granny made the boy help her when she sold her famous cure for the common cold. "Gold Dust," she called it, so people paid a lot.

Jack could tell you how it made your head heat up, how your ears caught fire, and your eyes and nose ran like steamy waterfalls till there was no more cold inside you. Of course, Granny's gold dust was nothing but a lot of hot mustard. And Jack would tell you that, too, for he was an honest boy.

Some folks wondered why he worked for Granny Trick. Well, fact was, Jack loved Skinny Bones, and as the boy grew up, the dog grew older. When the boy was finally big enough to run away, the dog was too old to limp to the next cactus. And Jack would never leave him. No, it was Granny that'd have to go, and Jack would have to be as clever as the devil himself to get her to do that.

As it happened, the devil was passing through one day, and hearing enough whooping and hollering to think he was nearly home, he stopped to look in Granny Trick's window.

The old lady was running this way and that, chasing the boy, waving an empty fry pan. Skinny Bones was hiding under the table; he'd gulped down one of Jack's lip-smacking golden pancakes.

"The devil take you!" Granny hollered. "The devil take you both!"

"Yoohoo, Granny!" said the devil.

The old lady was a mite surprised to find him standing at her door. When the devil thanked her for Jack, she took back her words. Flinging her arms around the boy, she cried, "No, no! Not my angel child!"

"And the mutt," said the devil.

Now Jack's eyes were big-around as the pancakes he flipped. He held on tight to Skinny Bones.

But the old lady said she wouldn't give up him or the dog, and everybody knew, even by hell's rules, the devil couldn't just take them. So the devil offered Granny a couple things in exchange—some of them right nice to have in a desert: a river, a well deep down to China, rain every Thursday.

"No deal," said Granny, closing the door on the devil's nose. "Not for one drop less than all the water in the world," she added, laughing at him for thinking she was fool enough to swap with somebody tricky as herself.

The devil skipped around to the window. "Lady, you got it!" he said. "Before the next full moon, I'll be around again to ask you to swap. I hope you can do the backstroke."

Then he reached in, snatched the last one of Jack's golden pancakes, and hurried off to find some rain.

Now Granny got just a wrinkle worried. She hmmm-hmmm-hmmm'd, then turned to the boy and said, "Better make me something that floats." She gave Jack some wood, barely enough for a small boat.

The boy hung the boat from the kitchen rafters. When it was stocked with food, he saw there wasn't any room for Skinny Bones—or him. And the boy started thinking.

Every night Granny slept in the little boat, hatchet by her side, ready to chop the ropes and sail out the door if the flood came. The boy lay below, thinking hard on what he and the dog might do.

The night before the full moon, rain started, tapping softly on Granny Trick's roof. She climbed into her boat, snuggled down all cozy and said, "I reckon tonight's the night."

Below her Jack made pancakes and set the table. "Tonight's the night," he whispered to Skinny Bones.

At quarter to twelve the devil showed up. He stood outside for a few minutes getting good and wet—for it was storming only on Granny's house.

When the boy opened
the door, the devil heard
the old woman snoring.
He saw her boat hanging
ready right above the
kitchen table. And he
knew Granny, high and
dry, wasn't going to be
scarified into any quick
deals.

"Shouldn't have been
so lazy about bagging
the wind and rain," he
muttered, then rubbed an
earlobe, turning up the
volume of the storm.

"I made us some pancakes," Jack shouted over the wind and rain. "In case you're hungry and the journey to hell is long."

"It's short, boy," the devil replied. But then he saw the extra-golden golden cakes. "They do look tempting," he said. Setting down at the table, he tucked a napkin around his chin and shoveled down a mouthful.

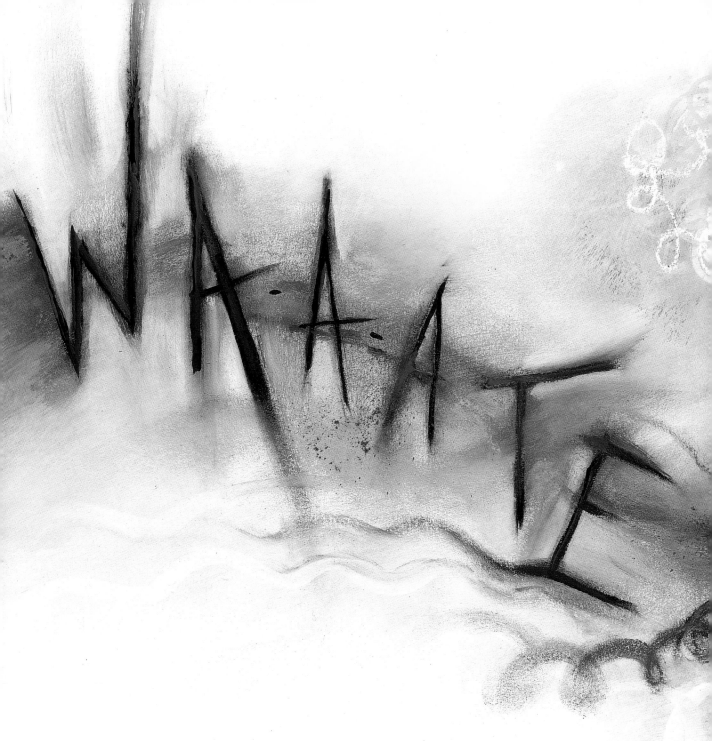

Next moment, the devil's eyes were bulging. His head heated up. His ears blew yellow smoke and his eyes and nose ran like steamy waterfalls. His throat burned, afire from those extra-golden mustard cakes.

"WATER! WATER!" the devil shouted.

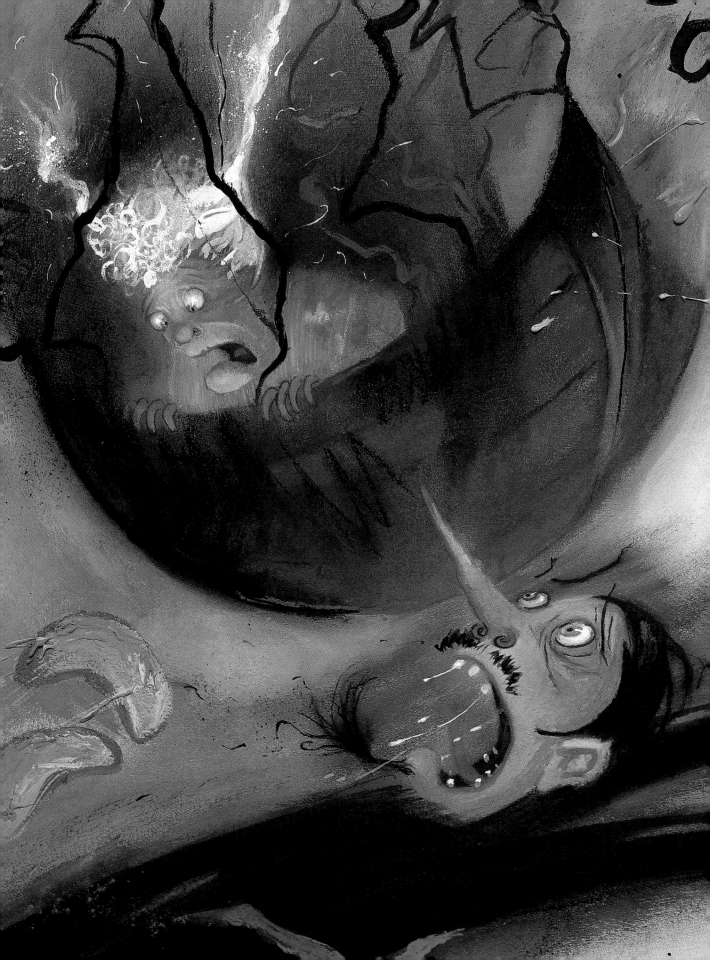

Up sat Granny Trick,
sure as sure the flood
had come.

Whack, whack, went
her hatchet.

Down came the boat.

Granny set sail on the devil's back.

Some say he ran all the way to hell with her. Whether that way is short or long, I can't say.

All I know is the boy and dog never saw the devil or Granny Trick again. And for a whole week after, pretty little desert flowers bloomed around their happy home.

For Marty and Theresa, with love —M.C.H.

AUTHOR'S NOTE: The long tradition of devil tales, which can be found in collections ranging from African American (*Uncle Remus*'s "Jacky-My-Lantern") to European (Grimms' "The Peasant and the Devil"), inspired this story: once again, the big trickster meets his match. While stirring up the plot, I added ingredients from other kinds of tales. The mustard trick appears in the thirteenth-century English fabliau *Dame Sirith*. The climactic device is found in one of the most famous and hilarious of Chaucer's *Canterbury Tales*, though we know it was used a century before him by a Flemish writer, and is believed to be older than that. How did such a concoction—as odd as one of Granny's—end up being baked in the Southwestern desert and served up like an American tall tale? I don't honestly know, except that I love tall tales. I hope you enjoy this one.

The artwork was done using gouache, gesso, and pastel on illustration board.

VIKING   Published by the Penguin Group
Penguin Books USA Inc., 375 Hudson Street, New York, New York 10014, U.S.A.
Penguin Books Ltd, 27 Wrights Lane, London W8 5TZ, England   Penguin Books Australia Ltd, Ringwood, Victoria, Australia
Penguin Books Canada Ltd, 10 Alcorn Avenue, Toronto, Ontario, Canada M4V 3B2
Penguin Books (N.Z.) Ltd, 182–190 Wairau Road, Auckland 10, New Zealand

Penguin Books Ltd, Registered Offices: Harmondsworth, Middlesex, England

First published in 1996 by Viking, a division of Penguin Books USA Inc.

Text copyright © Mary Claire Helldorfer, 1996   Illustrations copyright © Elise Primavera, 1996
All rights reserved

LIBRARY OF CONGRESS CATALOGING-IN-PUBLICATION DATA
Helldorfer, Mary Claire.   Jack, Skinny Bones, and the golden pancakes/
M. C. Helldorfer ; illustrated by Elise Primavera. p. cm.
Summary: Jack joins up with Granny Trick's dog Skinny Bones
and together they outwit both the wily old lady and the devil himself.
ISBN 0-670-86006-9   [1. Folklore.] I. Primavera, Elise, ill.   II. Title.
PZ8.1.H3795Jac 1996   398.22—dc20   [E] 95-46306 CIP AC

Set in Journal Text Bold   Manufactured in China   10 9 8 7 6 5 4 3 2 1